Tilli
Comes to
Texas

By Evelyn Oppenheimer

Illustrated by
Mary Haverfield

Hendrick-Long Publishing Company
Dallas, Texas

Designed by Carolyn Andres

Oppenheimer, Evelyn.
  Tilli Comes to Texas.

    Summary: Tilli, a Blue Spruce tree from Canada, relates her experiences after she
arrives in Texas to be a Christmas tree.
    [1. Trees — Fiction.   2. Christmas — Fiction]
I. Haverfield, Mary, ill.   II. Title
PZ7.06216Ti 1986   [E]   86-3089
ISBN 0-937460-21-4

Tilli
Comes to
Texas

My name is Tillicum, but you may call me Tilli for short and because it sounds more friendly.

Tillicum is an Indian word, and I come from a great country in the north where there are many Indians. But I am not an Indian.

I am a tree, a Blue Spruce, and my family told me never to forget that because it means something special.

Our home was in Canada, and I grew up in the part of Canada that goes toward the sunset. It has the name British Columbia because it is too big to have just one name.

It was a beautiful, wonderful home where I could look up and see the mountaintops shining icy white in the sun and moonlight. And I could look down and see lakes of green and blue water with birds forever flying and always knowing where they were going. At night the stars were everywhere watching over us.

My father was Mr. Blue Spruce,
and of course my mother was Mrs. Blue
Spruce. I had many sisters and brothers,
all of them older, but everyone said that
I was the best looking. The birds said
so. And the deer said so. And once

even a moose said so. And several times
I heard the Indians say so as they
walked by so quietly.

But I never felt proud. Only
thankful. What I wanted was to be as
good as I looked. I held myself very
straight. I said my prayers to the Great

Spirit who holds all the earth in His hands. I listened to His voice in the winds that blew over me and in the rolling thunder and in the silver waterfall near me, and I learned not to be afraid of anything. Except one thing.

Fire.

I had felt the smoke once when it came like a dark cloud from where a forest was burning after lightning struck and the trees were dying. That made me very sad and frightened.

B

ut all the rest of the time I was happy. Especially when the snow came and nestled all around me. I held its softness in my arms, and its whiteness made me look bluer and greener than ever. Then I would toss my branches and laugh and know what a fine spruce tree I was getting to be.

When the snow melted, I could feel the cool water going down to my roots, and that is a very good feeling if you are a tree.

Home is so very important to a tree, because you never leave it, unless something happens.

I had no way of knowing that something was about to happen when I saw the strange men coming up the mountain the day that began my great adventure.

They were talking about a very faraway place in the United States called Texas. They were in the Christmas tree business, and one of them had an ax. He looked at me.

"There's a perfect one," he said. "Perfect balance and not too big and not too small. Just right."

It all happened so quickly that it did not hurt — much. I am a Blue Spruce, and my family is very brave. If only there had been time to tell them goodbye, but one of the men picked me up in his arms and carried me down the mountain to a truck filled with other trees. I tried to be polite and greet them, but I was too excited about riding in a truck for the first time.

That ride was just the beginning. After that I was put on a boat and then a train that took me across the United

States. I stayed so excited at seeing all this strange country that there was no time to be lonely. Once on a railroad siding in the desert an odd little tree introduced himself to me and said he was a Mesquite.

The Americans were all very kind and gentle with me. They would say, "Well, what do you know — here's a real Blue Spruce! Some Christmas tree!" I wished my family could have heard them.

Finally I came to a big city where I saw trees I had never seen before. They were called Magnolias. I was in Texas.

I was taken to a very fine store, and people came and looked at me more than at the other trees. They said that I cost more money than the others. But one man and lady with a little boy and girl did not care how much I cost. They said that they had been to Canada once and knew my family background.

They bought me and put me in a very splendid automobile all open at the top and took me home. It was a beautiful house, and I was put right by a big window where I could look out and see a garden and swimming pool.

They kept talking about Christmas and what a special day it would be now that I was there.

They had very funny names. The little boy was called Bud. The little girl was Sis. The mother and father were just Honey.

They put the prettiest things on
me. Bright and shiny things and
something they called snow that looked
like snow but did not feel like it. Then
they put a star on my head. All their
friends came to see and admire me.

The only trouble was that their house was too warm, but I did not complain. A Blue Spruce is always very brave.

The night before Christmas was wonderful, with music from a magic box and everybody singing. At last Bud and Sis went to bed, and then Mr. and Mrs. Honey brought in the man I had heard so much about — Santa Claus.

He and I liked each other right away. He said that we were partners in the biggest job in the world — making people forget their troubles and be happy.

Boxes with bright ribbons and bows were put all around me. I could not sleep a wink, because I had to guard them all.

It was hardly light next morning when all the family came running into my room, and you never saw nor heard such happy people as they laughed and

shouted and opened all the beautiful boxes and took out the wonderful things in them — dolls and balls and fishing rods and toy cars and books and jackets and ties and skates and things that even a Blue Spruce does not know about.

They stayed with me all day, and
I felt just like a king or queen —
something very grand and important.

Next day the mother and father
began talking about New Year's, and
Bud and Sis cried and said I had to stay
there. I wanted to stay with them too.

And so we all stayed together
and played and were so very happy. Until
the day after New Year's.

Then the father, who said he had a headache, took me out while the children were away. He took me back to the alley and put me in a big garbage can. Really I was heartbroken. I knew that I had done a good job of giving happiness and that this was no way to treat me. Besides, I knew how Bud and Sis would cry. And besides that, what good of any kind can you do in a garbage can?

I had to make myself be as brave as only a Blue Spruce can be.

Then suddenly the wind began blowing out of the north, very cold. In Texas they call that a "norther." It felt like an old friend, bringing me messages from home. And when night came, other friends came too, hundreds and thousands and millions of them...

Snowflakes!

They covered the garbage can and
made it look like a great tree trunk.
They spread a lovely white carpet all
over the alley until nothing ugly could
be seen. They filled my arms and
warmed my heart, whispering of home.

After a while I began to feel so sleepy. In my sleep I began to dream of another wonderful Christmas. And do you know what happened? I dreamed myself right out of that garbage can and all the way across those miles and miles and miles until I was home again with all my family in our beautiful mountain forest white with snow.

That is what you can do if you are a Blue Spruce and really dream. After Christmas.

But I woke up at a touch that trembled so that it almost shook me. A boy stood there, shivering. He had no coat, not even a sweater. His eyes told me that he had had no Christmas at all.

Very carefully he picked me up and carried me a long way through the night to his home. It was a very poor little place with almost nothing in it.

On a cot lay his mother under a torn old blanket. Her hands were shaking, and her face was pale with sickness. A lamp was the only light, and it was broken and propped against a wall.

"See!" the boy said, all his worry in his voice, "I found this little tree that people had thrown out. A Christmas tree. I knew I would find one. I will make a fire now to get you warm and well again!"

If only I could have run away. But a tree cannot do that.

Then I remembered two things.
First, that my job was to give
Happiness, and what could bring greater
Happiness than to give this boy and his
mother the warmth they needed?

Second, I remembered that a Blue
Spruce is brave — even brave enough to
be cut up into firewood.

But suddenly the mother got up and came to me and touched me gently. Her hands were no longer shaking, and her eyes were soft and glowing, and her smile was wonderful.

"Oh no, dear," she said. "We must keep it a while yet. How marvelous that you found it! It's a Blue Spruce, and we used to have them at home where I grew up and met your father so many years ago. It makes me so happy just to look at it that I feel better already. Much, much better and all warm inside. See?"

Ｓhe turned and put her arms around the boy, and they laughed and cried together.

I stood very still, for that is what a tree does when it is listening to Happiness.

The
End